W9-CCM-657

A Home for Little Turtle

Ariane Chottin
Adapted by Deborah Kovacs
Illustrations by Pascale Wirth

Reader's Digest Kids
Pleasantville, N.Y. – Montreal

One bright, sunny day, a little turtle hid in a corner of the garden feeling sorry for herself. "I wish I didn't live inside this big clunky shell," she sighed, munching on a lettuce leaf.

"Hello, little turtle!" said a big gray cat, bounding into the garden. "I'm going for a walk in the woods."

"May I come, too?" asked the turtle hopefully.

"Sorry," said the cat. "With that big shell on your back, you could never keep up with me!" And with that, the cat leaped over the garden wall and was gone.

"I'll just go for a walk by myself then," said the turtle. She headed down the road toward the forest. By and by, a frisky red fox ran up to her.

"Hello, little turtle!" he said. "Where are you going?"

"I'm looking for a new home," said the turtle. "Where do you live?"

"I live in a warm burrow with my mama and papa and the rest of my family," said the little fox.

"You're lucky," sighed the lonely little turtle as she continued on her way.

Farther along, the turtle met a pretty gray dove. "Hello, little turtle," said the dove. "Where are you going?"

"I'm looking for a new home," said the little turtle. "Where do you live?"

With her delicate wing, the dove pointed to a nest in the hollow of a nearby bush. "I live with my babies in a nest lined with soft down."

"You're lucky," sighed the little turtle, thinking about the hard shell on her back.

As the turtle continued on her walk, her shell began to feel heavier and heavier. Just then, a little pink muzzle covered with whiskers appeared from a hole in the ground. It was a little mole.

"Hello, little turtle," said the mole. "Where are you going?"

"I'm looking for a new home," said the turtle, glancing around for the mole's house. "Where do you live?"

"I live deep in the earth, far away from light and noise," said the mole. "My home is an underground palace of huge rooms."

"You're lucky," said the little turtle. "I wish I had a fine home like that."

The turtle continued on her way and soon passed a wheat field bright with red poppies.

"Hello, little turtle!" squeaked a field mouse. "Welcome to my house!"

"Where do you live?" asked the little turtle.

"Here among the wheat stalks," answered the nimble little mouse. "See, my house is a little ball of straw hanging in the wheat. It's so light it sways with the wind."

"You're lucky," said the little turtle from under her heavy shell.

The turtle shuffled away sadly. Soon she reached the top of a hill overlooking the little garden. As she watched the sun beginning to set, something furry brushed against her.

"It's you!" said the little turtle to the gray cat. "I finally caught up with you!"

"I'm going back to the garden now," said the cat. "Do you want to come?"

"I might as well," said the little turtle. "I couldn't find what I was looking for."

The cat dashed on ahead as the little turtle started back down the hill.

Slowly, slowly, the turtle returned to the garden. By the time she got there, night had fallen. The garden was lit by a thin sliver of moon. "I wish I didn't have this shell on my back," she began to cry. "I wish I lived in a real home."

A kind voice behind her spoke up.
"What's wrong, little turtle?" called the voice.

The turtle turned to see a snail perched on a leaf. "I'm sad because I don't have a real home," said the turtle. "The fox has a warm burrow. The dove has a soft nest. The mole has an underground palace. The field mouse has a straw ball. They're all so lucky, and I have nothing at all."

"No, you are the lucky one, little turtle," said the snail. "You're like me. Our shells are our homes. We can travel the world, sleeping under the stars, and always have a place to call home."

"I never thought about my shell that way," said the little turtle, suddenly feeling much better about herself. She was proud that her special home would protect her, no matter where she was.

Beneath a twinkling canopy of stars, the turtle and the snail slept together, shell to shell. The two friends dreamed of the places they would visit and the adventures they would share, never far from home.

Turtles like to eat all kinds of plants, worms, and tiny fish. They often live in gardens where they feast on lettuce leaves.

Turtles like to keep warm. But when the sun gets too hot, they seek shade under leaves and rocks.

Even though some turtles may look alike, every turtle's shell has a different pattern. This is similar to the way every person has different fingerprints.